DUCK
ON HOLIDAY

Jenny Tyler
Illustrated by Stephen Cartwright

Consultant: Betty Root
Reading and Language Information Centre
University of Reading, England
Edited by Heather Amery

Duck goes to the beach.

First he finds a rock pool.

Then he goes for a swim

and he sails on a boat.

Duck gets dry and has a drink.

Then he builds a sandcastle.

But Dog's ball knocks it down.

Dog shares his ice cream with Duck.

Duck and Dog ride on a merry-go-round.

Duck's holiday is over.

It is time to go home.